ALL I'VE GOT

by: Marissa Ann

Credits:
Cover Design by: Francessca PR & Designs
Editor: Rachel Goldman

ASIN:
ISBN-13: 978-1-7365798-9-3

About: *All I've Got*

I've spent my whole life in the spotlight. From star athlete in high school to the major leagues in the blink of an eye.

When an injury suddenly ends my career, I return home a celebrity. The problem with that is I don't want to be a celebrity. I want to teach kids, give them the chances that I had when I was kid.

My best friend gets me the job I've always wanted. Coaching the Little League All Star team from his hometown. So I pack up and move as fast as I can to live my dream working with kids.

One in particular catches my eye but local politics might prevent him from becoming the star player I know he can be. That young man is not the only one that catches my eye in this town though.

Can his mom overcome the years of abuse and gossip this town has piled on her? I don't know, but I'm going to give it all I've got to make her mine.

Chapter 1

Becky

"I'm going to be late for work. Do you have everything in your bag?" I ask Max as we get into the car.

He never looks up from his phone, just shakes his head as if I can hear him.

"Max, I asked you a question." I patiently say.

"I answered." He huffs, having been interrupted from his perusal of his video.

"No, you didn't. Shaking your head is not an answer." I turn left onto the street that leads to his friend Tommy's house.

"Yes, mom, I got everything." He calmly answers finally while putting his phone away.

"I'll see you later when Mr. Scott drops you off at the diner."

I pull up into the Scott's driveway and watch as Mrs. Scott steps out on the porch giving me a little wave.

"Love you, Mom!" Max shouts as he jumps out, running to the porch.

I wave back at Mrs. Scott before pulling back out onto the road. Harry, my boss at the diner, is going to be a little ill about my running late but his wife, Martha, always calms him down.

He's not a bad guy really. He treats me like the daughter he and his wife never had. They were never able to have children. While they always seemed okay with that, I still get the feeling that it saddens them.

Growing up in this town was hard for me. My family didn't have money, not even to keep the lights on from month to month. Harry and Martha took me under their wing even back then. Always making sure that I had something to eat and clean clothes to wear to school. My mom never even noticed.

The year I turned sixteen is when things went from bad to worse. That's the year that Max's dad took an interest in me. Craving attention that I never received before, I soaked it up like a sponge never really knowing that all James wanted was to get in my pants. Once he had that, I no longer existed for him.

Once he found out about Max, he spread lies all over town about seeing me at the local bar just outside of town giving it up to every trucker that happened through. After going through all of that, I never told the truth about who Max's father was.

The only one I'll ever owe an explanation to is Max. When the day comes and he asks, I'll tell him the truth about all of it.

Pulling up at the diner, I park the car and head inside, slipping my apron on as I walk through the back.

"There you are. You're late! Thought we'd be short handed." Harry growls but I smile at him, kissing his cheek as I pass by. "Don't think to butter me up, missy!" Although he sounds harsh, he smiles as I go to the front to find Martha at the counter.

"There's my sweet girl! Can you go take that couple in the back order while I ring up this gentleman?" She asks in her sweet voice.

"Yes ma'am." I answer as I get to work.

Brian

Getting to the ball park where the all star team is practicing, I stay out of sight just to watch for a few minutes. This is the best way to catch things the kids may need a little work on.

One boy in particular stands out from the rest. He seems to have a natural talent for the game. As he steps up to the plate though I notice his stance is a little off. It's not a huge issue as long as it is corrected. I have the perfect solution for it in one of my bags.

It's a stance trainer. There's quite a few on the market but they truly do work. When you practice standing the correct way, eventually your body will do it automatically.

Sonny Richardson finally notices me before anyone else does. He's the reason I was invited to coach this all-star team. We've been friends since we first met in college. While my baseball career took off, he finished up law school.

About a year ago, I came down wrong on one of my knees during a game. It messed it up pretty good. Even after surgery I knew I would never be able to go back to playing the game I loved.

Sonny is the one that planted the seed into my head about teaching the game to the younger generation. Not that I needed a job or anything. I've made enough during my short career and invested it well so that I am set for life.

"I was wondering when you would get here." He says, walking up beside me.

"I've been here for a few minutes. I just wanted to watch the boys without them knowing that I'm here already. I figure they'll try too hard to impress me when I really just need to watch for anything they may need more work on." I explain, still watching the boy at the plate.

"That's actually a good idea." He laughs a little.

"Who's the kid at the plate? I noticed him as soon as I got here. He's got some natural talent." I ask with interest.

"That would be Max Ross. He's a damn fine little ball player, but I wouldn't count on him staying on the team." He comments with the shake of his head.

"Why is that?" I ask, wondering if there is a problem with the boy's home life.

"The boosters will cut anyone who can't afford the fees for the all star league. His mom works at a diner. Her name is Rebeccah but she goes by Becky. The other moms will take great delight in her not being able to afford it." He explains as we continue to watch.

"So you brought me into a vipers nest." I laugh.

"You can handle them. Personally, I hope she does get all the funds to cover his fees. Serve those bitches right. He's the best player on the team as it is, although they would try to argue that fact."

"Why not just do fundraisers to help the kids get all the money?" I ask but I am sure I already know the answer.

I know these types of people because it's what I grew up with. My family was one of the poorest in my hometown. I was ridiculed constantly at school but I absolutely dominated the baseball field.

"That would be what others would do. But if they did that, then it's possible anyone could be let on the team." He confirms my suspicion.

"People are jackasses." I growl.

"You are certainly right about these jackasses." He whispers back.

Chapter 2
Becky

About an hour into my shift a few of the women I went to school with walk in. As much as I would like to ignore them, I'm the only waitress here at the moment.

"Can I take your order?" I say as politely as I can.

"Three hamburgers with fries on the side and tea to drink. Try not to get your greasy hair in it." Karen quickly says with a sneer.

Not wanting to give her the reaction I know she is looking for, I walk away from the table to give Harry the order.

After I deliver their food, I walk around wiping down the tables trying to ignore their conversation. They do this about once a week. They'll come in here just to run their mouths hoping I'll say something back. I learned a long time ago that showing anger of any kind puts a huge smile on Karen and her friends' faces.

"She is so nasty. I really can't imagine what Mr. and Mrs. Crawly were thinking, hiring her to work here. She probably blows every new customer that comes through in the back alley." They talk loud enough for me to hear but I continue working hoping they don't stay long.

"Didn't your husband show an interest in her back in high school senior year?" Catherine asks Karen.

"Boys are allowed a few indiscretions while still young. Besides, it was well known even then that she was an easy lay. We can't expect young men to just ignore that all the time." Karen says with a confidence that even I don't believe.

"Of course not. If she was giving it away, she deserved what she got." Megan throws into the conversation not wanting to be left out.

After they finish with their food, they don't stay too much longer before leaving. I'm just thankful not too many other patrons came in while they were here although quite a few have been known to come to my defense when hearing the remarks coming from those three.

"Those three still need a good switch to their backside." Martha says as we watch them walk to their cars.

"Well if anyone decides to do the switching make sure they record it. We can post it online and become famous." We both laugh at the thought.

"Oh I was supposed to tell you that Sara Richardson was needing someone who could clean her office building on the weekends. She thought you would be perfect for the job." Martha says.

"That'll be great! I need the extra right now to cover Max's fees with the all-star team." I smile at the thought.

"Hey mom!" Max shouts, walking through the door.

"Hey kiddo. How was practice?" I ask, grabbing a quick hug. Luckily he's not yet reached the age where all public displays of my affection are off limits.

"It was awesome! The new coach that used to play for the Mets was there. He's so awesome! He took time to show me the right placement for my feet at the plate. I'm supposed to practice standing that way every day until next practice." Smiling at his enthusiasm, I guide him to a booth to sit in until my shift is over.

I go to the back to place an order for him so that he can eat. When it's ready, I pick it up and head back to his booth. When I do, I notice a man I've never seen before sitting in the booth with him. Panic rises in my chest as I hurry over.

"Hey mom, this is Coach Brian." Max says when I walk up, placing his food in front of him.

Coach Brian stands up holding his hand out to me. Taking it, I shake his hand.

"Nice to meet you Mrs..."

"Ross. It's just Miss though." I smile in greeting. "It's nice to meet you as well. Max here has been super excited about you coming to coach the all-star team."

"Yeah, working with kids is great." He smiles back, finally letting go of my hand.

"Can I get you something to eat?" I grab my order pad waiting.

After giving me his order, I get back to my job as more people come in for the dinner hour.

Brian

I sit with Max while eating dinner and easily talk baseball with him. He's not just interested in the things I have done, he truly wants to learn the ins and outs of baseball.

I watch Becky from the corner of my eye while she is busy working. The woman is absolutely gorgeous with the kindest eyes. She's probably the first one to not automatically flirt with me like the other moms did during practice.

I've actually debated making it mandatory that all parents must leave while practice is in session. If I have to put up with those women again, I'm likely to quit. Their snide remarks about Max during practice had me gritting my teeth so much that I've probably broken several.

"So, do you like school?" I ask him between bites.

"Only the classes that I don't have with Luke." He grumbles with his mouth full.

"You talking about the same Luke from the team?" I ask, my interest spiking.

He just shakes his head in answer this time instead of trying to talk around his food.

"You want to tell me why?" I whisper to him.

He looks around until he sees that his mom is behind the counter before turning back to look at me.

"You aren't going to tell my mom are you?" He says with a serious expression.

"I promise. It'll just be between us guys." Although I promise him, I know that if it's too bad I will have to tell his mom.

"He likes to call me a bastard and gets the other kids to say it too." He shrugs like it's not that big of a deal.

"I'm guessing you know what the word means?" I ask him.

"Yeah, I know what it means but I don't care. Not really. I watch the other boys at school with their dads and some of them aren't that nice. Except Mr. Scott, he never yells at Tommy or me. Even if we mess up." I listen as he explains it all from his perspective and can tell that while he's had it rough, deep down he's a smart little boy that will go far in life.

"My dad doesn't yell either. Not even when I mess up." I smile at him as we finish eating.

A little while later, I say my goodbyes to Max before walking up to the counter to pay for my tab.

"Leaving already? I hope your food was to your liking." Becky greets me at the cash register.

"It was very good actually. I'm just going to head home. The movers moved everything in but I only just got here this morning so I'm a little tired." I smile, handing her my credit card.

"Here you go." She says, handing me the card and a receipt.

"Would you like to have coffee with me sometime?" I smile hoping that she will agree. A woman hasn't turned my head in a really long time. This one, not batting her lashes at me, intrigues the hell out of me.

"I don't think that would be a very good idea." She answers, looking around as if to see if anyone heard.

"Why wouldn't it be?" I ask.

"I'm not that kind of woman. Thank you Coach Brian. Have a good night." She firmly says before walking away.

Accepting the no for now, I stick the receipt in my pocket as I head out the door. I'll get her to have coffee with me, I vow to myself. Any woman that doesn't automatically turn on her charms from looking at me is definitely worth a second look. Even a third and fourth look.

Chapter 3
Brian

It took a few days to get all of my stuff unpacked from the boxes. I'm just finishing up putting the plates up in the cabinet when I notice it's time to head over to Sonny's place.

He and his wife, Sara, invited me to dinner tonight at their house. He warned me that the Mayor would be there with his wife as well as a few other people.

They'll want to talk about the boys and which ones I think will need to be cut from the team. While they have a lot of say in who stays or goes, ultimately it is up to the coach. Since I am the coach, I'm prepared to butt heads with whomever I need to.

I'm walking up to Sonny's door about fifteen minutes later.

"I was beginning to wonder if you were going to leave me to all these wolves by myself." Sonny whispers, opening the door to invite me in.

"I seriously thought about it." I whisper back.

"The mayor's wife is a pain in the ass so watch her." He whispers just before we walk into his dining room.

"Brian, good to see you!" Mayor Hall exclaims, shaking my hand. "This is my gorgeous wife, Karen." He introduces the lady standing beside him.

"Luke's parents, right?" I ask, looking at them as I remember Max talking about Luke being a bully.

"That's right. Isn't he just the best ball player?" Karen smiles wide but I don't agree with her assessment of his abilities as a ball player.

There are several on the team that are far better at the sport. Part of the sport is being a team player that isn't a bully to others.

"We were just discussing who we thought you may want to cut from the team. The all stars can only have the best players after all." Mayor Hall comments.

"I think the Ross boy should be the first to go." Karen curls her lip and I no longer wonder where Luke gets his bullying ways from.

"The Ross boy is probably the best player on the team. Why would I want to cut him?" I ask with defiance.

"You can't be serious? Besides, his mother will never be able to pay the fees needed." Karen gives me a hard look.

"Now Karen, Brian is right. The boy is an amazing player on the field." Mayor Hall tries to convince his wife.

"Why do you always take up for him?" I hear her whisper heatedly. The Mayor seems to squeeze her hand hard and she sits quietly for the rest of the evening.

I wonder briefly why Karen Hall seems to dislike Max and his mom. After we eat dinner, I stay as long as needed to not be rude before I say goodnight and leave.

I really dislike those who believe they are better than others and that is exactly how Karen thinks. It's a huge sigh of relief as I back out of the driveway, heading back towards town.

Thinking I'll stop by the store and grab some stuff for sandwiches, I pull into the local market that is still open.

This being such a small town, most of the shops and stores close earlier than I am used to. There's only a few other cars in the lot, hopefully I can grab what I need before they lock the doors.

Walking inside, I see only one cashier at the front.

"We close in ten minutes." She says with a polite smile.

"I won't be long." I reply back, grabbing a small basket.

As I turn a corner heading towards the meat department, I catch sight of Becky pushing a shopping cart.

I stop to watch her for a minute smiling at the way she seems to study everything before she puts it into her basket.

The thought that she is probably checking the price and calculating it all up zips through my mind causing me to look at her a little more closely.

Honestly, I think the woman is beautiful although she does look as though she could use a few more meals.

She finally looks up as if feeling my eyes on her. I can't stop the smile that takes over my face as I walk towards her.

"Hey." She says when I reach her side.

"Hello. Do you normally shop for groceries this late?" I ask.

"If I can. I like when there aren't so many people in the store." She says.

"And no chance to run into the Mayor's wife?" I ask, grinning.

"Exactly." She makes a face causing me to laugh out loud.

"Where's Max?" I ask, looking around for the kid that is normally always with his mom except at practices.

"He went to his friend's house. I'm supposed to pick him up on my way home. I should get up to the check out before they shut down the register." She says quickly, turning away.

I watch as she walks away. The woman intrigues the hell out of me to no end.

Moving on, I grab the rest of the stuff that I need, making my own way to the front of the store.

Becky is still in line, trying to use the credit card machine. She gives me a polite smile as I set my own groceries on the belt.

"This says you only have eighty four dollars left on your food stamp card. You'll have to pay the thirty dollar difference." The cashier says to Becky with a huff.

Staying silent, I see Becky's eyes cut over towards me as she begins digging in her purse.

"Um. Can I take a few things off please?" Becky asks, her face turning red in embarrassment.

"Just add my stuff to it and I'll pay the difference." I speak up. The cashier looks at me as if I have lost my mind.

"No. I'll just take a few things off. Thank you though." Becky's voice becomes hard and unyielding again towards me.

I wait for them to finish up and I watch her walk out the door with her bags.

"I don't know why people like that can't just check their balances ahead of time." The cashier huffs again but turns silent from my eyes narrowing to slits.

"People like that are hard working and kind." I say through gritted teeth after I pay, grabbing my bags and heading for the door.

"Fucking people and their narrow minded bullshit." I talk to myself as I head to my car.

"Hey, sorry about what happened in there." I hear from my left, looking over I see Becky standing next to her car.

"It's all good. I overstepped. I'm the one that should be apologizing to you." I say politely.

"You were trying to be kind and I'm not exactly used to that. Usually if someone is being kind, then they want something from me." She shrugs her shoulder.

"I don't want anything from you Becky. Well...I do but I don't." I grin.

"What does that even mean?" She laughs, shaking her head.

"It means, I don't expect you to do anything but I am still hoping that you will have dinner with me." She laughs again, shaking her head. "Is that a no?" I ask.

"It's definitely a no." Her smile is huge when she says it this time.

She doesn't wait to see if I say anything else before getting into her car and driving away.

I'm still standing there grinning like a fool as I watch her tail lights fade into the dark.

I'll wear her down if it's the last thing I do. I think to myself, getting into my own car.

Becky

Sunday mornings at the diner are a little slower as people tend to trickle in all day instead of just during the rush hours.

Max stays in a booth in the back playing on his handheld game Martha and Harry gave him last year for his birthday. The game they got him for it, is of course a baseball game.

Baseball seems to be the only thing he studies these days. Even the videos he watches on YouTube are how to perfect his swing or curve ball.

I don't mind. It's great he has something at his age he is already passionate about. He's a lot more different than me in that regard. I'm an adult and still have no idea what to do with my life.

Around lunch time, I get a little bit busier as customers come in for the Sunday lunch special. By the time I look up again, Couch Brian is sitting with Max in the back.

"Hey, Can I get you anything? I'm sorry I didn't see you come in." I ask, walking up to the table.

"It's okay, you were kind of swamped when I walked in so I thought I would just sit with Max here." He smiles over at my son.

He turns his smile back to me but it seems to get a little bit wider showing a dimple on one side that is cute as hell.

Clearing my throat, I look back down to my order pad.

"What would you like to eat?" I ask but when he doesn't immediately answer, I look back up and am surprised at the look on his face which seems to say he'd like to eat me. I can feel my face heat up. He seems to notice exactly what he is doing to me.

"I'll take the special. For now." He murmurs and I hurry towards the kitchen to put his order in. Plus I need a minute in the restroom to cool down. Is the air not working?

Brian

She's beautiful when she blushes. I think to myself as I watch her hurry to the back.

"You like my mom, huh?" Max asks and I turn to see that he is watching me.

"Yeah, I guess I do. Is that okay?" I ask, wondering what he will say but all he does is shrug his shoulders before going back to his game.

"Just don't make her cry. I don't like it when she cries." He whispers a few minutes later, making my heart trip up.

"Someone's made your mom cry before?" I ask gently.

"Yeah, sometimes but I don't know who. She always cries at night in her room when she thinks I'm asleep." This kid doesn't miss much where his mom is concerned.

"I promise not to make her cry, if you'll do something for me." I say, getting his full attention.

"What do you need me to do?" He asks.

"I brought these so that you can practice your stance. They help to do that and are very effective. You can take these home with you and give them back at the end of the season." I explain, pulling out the stance trainer I brought with me in my bag.

"Awesome! Thanks Coach! I've been watching videos trying to get it right but these are amazing!" He says excitedly, holding them close to his chest as if given the best prize in the world.

"You're more than welcome. If you need any extra training any other time you can call me and we will put in some work in the field." I offer.

"That'll be great, Coach. Thanks!" Max says with a wide smile.

"Here you go." Becky says, setting a plate in front of me.

"Look mom, Coach Brian let me borrow a stance trainer!" He holds it up to show his mom with a wide smile.

"That's great sweetie!" She smiles widely at him.

"Would you and Max like to get pizza tonight?" I ask quickly before she can walk away again.

"Cool! Can we mom?" Max looks up at her with pleading eyes.

I can tell she wants to turn me down flat but Max being excited about the prospect is stopping her from doing so.

"Completely my treat. We can go to that place on the other side of town that has an arcade inside it." I raise my brows hoping she will say yes.

"Please mom? I've never been to Gamez Pizza before." Max pleads.

"Okay, but I don't get off until six." She finally gives in with a sigh.

"Not a problem. I can pick both of you up here at six." I smile widely at her.

She's an enigma. Not one to fawn all over me because of who I am. I like that about her plus the fact that I can tell she takes very good care of her son. They are both very close. That's a huge plus in my book.

Chapter 4
Becky

At around five thirty, I'm wondering what I was thinking to accept his offer but I already know why I did. Max wanted so badly to go, I couldn't tell him no.

It's so rare that I'm able to afford to do those kinds of things for him. He's never asked as if he knows I can't afford it and never seems upset by it. I, however, do get upset about it. I want to give him more in life.

So we will go tonight with Brian and both enjoy ourselves. He does seem like a nice man but I fell for that before only to find out later it was just a bet to sleep with me.

"Hey, mom, are you almost done? Coach is here." Max jumps up and down in the kitchen as I am finishing up some of the dishes for Martha.

"You two go ahead. We'll finish up here." Martha says with a smile.

"Are you sure?" I ask.

"Yep. Get that boy to the arcade before he jumps out of his skin." She laughs watching Max race back out the door.

I go to the back to wash up and to try to settle the nervousness I feel in my stomach. It's not like this is a date or anything. Right?

Walking outside, I see Brian and Max standing beside a car in the parking lot so I head in their direction.

"Here you go." Brian says, holding the front passenger door open for me.

"Thank you." I say, taking a seat inside.

I honestly thought he'd have some kind of fancy sports car or something since he was a well known ball player. Instead it's just a regular kind of car. Brand new but still not what you would think a guy like him would drive.

Max talks non-stop all the way to the pizza place. Pulling up into their parking lot you can tell that it is packed this evening. I figured it would be, which is the cause of some of the nervousness I feel. What if someone says something nasty to Brian about me? He probably wouldn't ask me out again, that's for sure.

Brian

We are seated in a booth towards the back closer to the arcade entrance. This place is really huge and is packed with kids running around everywhere.

I made sure to buy a hundred dollars worth of tokens for Max as we walked in. Becky looked like her eyes would bug out at the amount and Max was extremely appreciative. It feels amazing to give something to a kid that really appreciates what he gets. He's a lot different than most kids these days.

As our drinks are delivered, I look over at Becky. She is so beautiful but I don't think she actually knows that she is. She doesn't wear makeup as far as I have seen and honestly, she doesn't need it. She's just naturally beautiful.

"He'll probably spend all of that within thirty minutes." She chuckles nervously.

"Then, we'll get a hundred dollars more." I smile at her.

"I don't want him getting used to that like it's an everyday thing." She looks hard at me.

"Becky, I seriously doubt he'd ever think like that. You have raised a truly great kid. Most kids are unappreciative of what others give to them. I don't think you have that to worry about."

I reach over, putting my hand over the top of hers on the table. She looks up at me quickly but doesn't try to pull away. I take that as a good sign.

We stay like that for several minutes until someone walks up to our table. Becky pulls her hand away quickly and I look up to see who interrupted us.

"Well hello Coach Brian. I'm surprised to see you here." She looks between Becky and I.

"Mrs. Hall." I say in greeting to Karen. "We brought Max to play in the arcade and get some pizza." I smile broadly, reaching over, grabbing Becky's hand again and lacing our fingers together.

Karen notices and seems to curl her lip a little.

"Yes, well, I bring Luke here every Sunday. He loves it." She says, still not speaking directly to Becky. "I see our food is at our table now. We'll see you at practice tomorrow." She turns on her heels and walks away without another word.

Becky starts to laugh behind her hand a little bit, trying hard to not laugh out loud.

"Why are you laughing?" I ask her seriously.

"They are going to eat you alive at practice tomorrow." She shakes her head. "If after that, you decide you don't really want to acknowledge me in public again, I'll understand." She says sadly trying to pull her hand away.

Gripping her hand tighter, I bring it to my lips and kiss the tips of her fingers.

"There is not a damn thing those people could say to me that would ever make me not want to speak to you. In public or otherwise." My statement and the look I give her, causes her to gasp. "Our food is here." I grin wide, turning to the server.

Becky

He was already starting to get to me but when he kissed my fingers, chills shot up my spine as butterflies took over my stomach. I feel a need deep inside of me that I haven't felt in a really long time.

We finally got Max back to the table to help us eat the pizza while it was still hot. Afterwards, we all played numerous games within the arcade.

Max beat me in the race car game we played together. Surprisingly, I finally tamped down my nerves and started to really enjoy the evening out.

"That was so much fun, Coach! Thank you for taking me!" Max says to Brian as he walks us to the door.

"I'm glad you enjoyed yourself. Maybe we can do it again soon." Brian says, ruffling my son's hair.

"Go on in and get ready for bed." I say to Max as I open our door.

"Goodnight Coach!" Max yells, running inside.

"Night Max! See you tomorrow!" Brian yells back before turning his eyes back to me.

Chill bumps raise up on my arms as I look back at him and I shiver.

"Thank you for tonight. You made him so happy." I murmur.

"You don't have to thank me. I enjoyed it. Thank you for agreeing to go." His dimple popping out with his smile.

"Well you kind of put me on the spot when you asked in front of him." I grin back, raising my eyebrow.

"If you weren't so stubborn, I wouldn't have had to use such tactics. But I'm glad now that I did so I won't apologize for it." He chuckles.

"You think I'm stubborn?" I ask seriously.

"Actually, I think someone in your past has hurt you and you are now too afraid to take any chances." He whispers, taking a step closer to me.

He reaches one hand up, cupping my chin tilting my head back to look deeper into my eyes.

"I see sadness in you but I also see fire. I'd like to see that fire unleash one day." He whispers even more softly.

Very slowly, he lowers his face closer to my own. The second his lips touch mine, I moan, unable to help myself.

Pushing myself even closer to him, I let him deepen the kiss. I feel as though I am on fire and a deep throbbing need begins deep within my core.

All too soon, he pulls away, still looking into my eyes.

"I'll see you tomorrow." He says gently before turning away back towards his car. Leaving me on my porch step, panting with want.

"Damn." I say out loud, feeling my lips with my fingertips.

Chapter 5
Brian

Damn, I think to myself as I remember the kiss between Becky and I last night. I'm hard as a rock within seconds of the thought.

If a kiss can have me acting this way, I can just imagine how it'll be if she were to ever let me touch her. The woman was absolutely perfect as far as I was concerned.

She didn't care about who I was or my money. She actually seemed to hate how easily I could drop so much money on tokens for Max to play the games at the arcade. I was raised by parents that taught me that money was only good for one thing, to spend it on those you cared about.

I could easily see myself falling for Becky and If I gave her time, I could make her fall in love with me as well. I already felt attached to her son Max. He was an amazing young man. Sweet, kind, considerate, all the things that most kids were not these days.

Which is why quite a few will be pissed off this evening when they find out that Max would not be cut from the team. Besides, he was the best player the team had.

Heading to the kitchen, I remember that I still haven't yet gone grocery shopping. Luckily, I brought coffee with me when I moved so I don't have to skip having a cup before heading out this morning.

I'll swing by the cafe for breakfast. Besides, not having groceries gives me another excuse to see Becky again. Hopefully, she's at work this morning. If she's not, I'll find a way to see her after practice. Even if I have to volunteer to take Max home myself.

Before I can head out the door, my phone rings. Looking down I see that it is my dad. With a smile, I answer.

"Well did you get all moved in?" My dad's gruff voice booms across the line.

"Yes, sir. All moved in. I've not gone grocery shopping yet though so I was just headed out to the local diner for some breakfast." I answer.

"Hmm, why do you sound happy about going to the diner?" He asks with a chuckle.

With his question I hear my mom in the background as she scrambles to get the other cordless phone from the bedroom.

"Did you meet someone?" Mom asks breathlessly like she ran to the phone.

"Geez, mom. You didn't have to run." Dad and I chuckle at the same time.

"Well, have you?" She demands.

"Sort of. Her son is on the team. Really great kid and an amazing ball player. You should see him dad. Natural talent like you wouldn't believe." I talk quickly.

"He's changing the subject, Dan." Mom huffs.

"I noticed, dear." He answers back.

"He's so hard-headed. Just like you Dan." Mom says.

"Like me? I know all too well he definitely gets that from his mother!" Dad lightly growls back.

"You two know I am still on the phone right?" I ask, shaking my head.

These two have always gone back and forth with each other, always in good fun. They are the best parents anyone could have in my own opinion.

Dad worked a lot when I was younger just to keep a roof over our heads but he always made a point to be there for anything important.

I remember mom staying up late on some nights waiting for him to come home from work just so she could warm his supper up for him. Dad would always tell her she should have gone to bed. That he was perfectly capable of warming up his food.

I know he loved that she continued to do so anyway despite his protests. I would often hear them talking and laughing for several hours until I finally fell asleep.

That's the kind of love I want in my life. I think I've found the perfect woman to have that with. I just need to convince her of it. The more I get to know her, the more I feel for her in my heart.

I stay on the phone with my parents for a few more minutes before heading out the door. They both promised to visit later next week. I can't wait to introduce them to Becky and Max. They'll fall in love with them just as I expect that I am doing as well.

Becky

The kiss I shared with Brian last night has been a huge distraction since I got up this morning and it hasn't gotten better since being at work. I've mixed up several orders this morning causing some of the regulars to give me a strange look.

I'm just finishing up cleaning one of the vacant tables when the door opens with a jingle from the bell. Looking up, I see Karen and James walking in.

My heart begins to hammer in my chest at the thought of having to serve the two of them. It's bad enough when Karen comes in with her friends but to have to deal with James is something I do not want to do.

I try to walk quickly to the back so that I can get Martha to wait on their table before they see me. I think I am home free until Karen opens her fat mouth.

"Well there she is." Karen says loudly.

Turning in their direction, I don't even look at James as I answer Karen.

"Just pick a table. I'll be right with you." I quickly say before walking through the door into the kitchen.

I try to control my breathing before a panic attack can take over my body.

"Are you okay dear?" Martha asks worriedly as she quickly moves to my side.

"The mayor and his wife are here." I answer looking up into her eyes.

"I'll take care of it. You go wash your face and take care of yourself before coming back out." She pats my cheek with a soft smile before walking out.

Once I am in the restroom, I splash water onto my face until I begin to feel normal again. I don't know why I still allow them to get to me this way. I'm just thankful that I don't have to share Max with them. Hopefully I never have to.

Feeling a lot better, I head back out to do my job but what I see over at Karen's table causes my heart to jump again.

Max is standing next to their table while James talks to him. Karen has a sour look on her face. My feet finally move, carrying me over to Max as quickly as possible.

"You are a really good ball player." I hear James say to him.

"Thank you sir. I'm going to be in the major leagues one day." Max says with a huge smile.

"That is a lofty goal, don't you think?" James asks, looking at Max before his eyes look up at me. "Becky. Your son here thinks he's going to play in the major league one day." His lip curls in disgust while looking at me.

"If that is his goal, then I have no doubt at all that he will make it one day. He's a team player. Bullies don't really make it in life." I smile back.

"What's that supposed to mean?" James turns fully in my direction as Karen gets a huge grin like she knows I am about to be put in my place.

"What she means is that your own son, Luke, is not a team player." I hear from behind me.

Looking back, I see Brian who smiles at me before putting his arm around my waist. I am so grateful for him at this moment. I'm afraid that I may actually fall in love with him.

"Careful Mr. Lewis or you could find yourself without a job." James growls.

"I highly doubt it, seeing as I have a contract that extends longer than your political seat. You may not even be reelected next year. Besides, if you try, I'll be forced to sue the town." Brian smiles, completely relaxed against me.

James and Karen both seem to be speechless, staring at Brian as if he has two heads. I can't stop the smile that spreads across my face.

"Are you getting off soon? I was hoping you would be at Max's practice today." Brian looks down into my eyes.

"I'm on the clock for ten more minutes but yes, I planned to go today. I have the check for Max's fees to give to Sonny." I look back at Karen as her eyes seem shocked that I have saved up the expense for the team.

"Max and I will wait for you in the car." He kisses the tip of my nose, glances over at James and Karen without a word and walks out the door with my son.

My heart flips in my chest. Yes, I definitely can fall for this man. I'm all smiles for the last ten minutes of my shift.

Chapter 6
Brian

For the past week, I have spent every moment possible with Becky and Max. It's been amazing. The day that Becky paid Max's fees with the team was especially awesome. The looks on those assholes' faces knowing that he would not be cut from the team filled me with absolute pride.

Tonight is the first night Becky has had off from work so we made dinner plans together. Max is staying the night with his friend Tommy.

I finally went shopping for groceries so that I could cook dinner for her in my new house. I had offered to pick her up but she insisted that she would drive over after dropping Max off.

I've just finished setting the table when my doorbell rings. Smiling in anticipation, I walk quickly to the door.

Swinging it open, I see the most beautiful woman I have ever seen.

"You look amazing." I whisper, grabbing her hand and pulling her to me for a deep kiss.

"Thank you." She answers breathily when I finally pull away.

"Dinner is ready if you are." I say, walking her into the kitchen.

"It smells amazing. You really cooked all of this?" She asks, looking at the table.

"I like to cook. I really got into cooking after my knee injury. Cooking shows and all that." I grin, shrugging my shoulder.

"Well, I'm certainly impressed." She smiles back, taking a seat.

We take our time over dinner. Talking about many different things. She's definitely got a brain and knows how to use it. I learn during our conversation that she would really like to get her business degree one day. I tell her that is something I could certainly see her accomplishing.

This woman is so perfect. She's perfect for me. I can't wait to introduce her to my parents this weekend. They will spoil her as if she were their own. I smile at the thought.

Becky

I was so nervous getting ready for tonight. Although we have spent everyday together for the past week, tonight is different because we will finally be completely alone together.

He's been in my dreams every night and I wake up filled with need and my clit throbbing, wanting attention.

After we finish eating, I help him to clean the kitchen back up. We work really well as a team and I am surprised that I easily find where everything goes back into the cabinet.

"Want to watch a movie?" He asks as I turn back towards him.

"What kind of movie?" I ask, curious about what type of movies he likes.

"Anything is good with me. There's several different rental apps on the TV we can browse through." He says, pulling out a bag of popcorn and putting it in the microwave. "The remote is on the table if you want to go ahead and see what you can find." He smiles at me.

I smile back as I walk by, heading into the den, finding the remote exactly where he said it would be.

Scrolling through the first app I find that they have the newest release of a series that I love. I leave it highlighted knowing my selection is probably going to surprise him.

A few minutes later, he walks in carrying the bowl of popcorn, taking a seat next to me on the couch.

"So what did you find?" He asks, looking over at me before looking back at the screen. "Really? That's what you want to watch?" He chuckles.

"What? Those are some awesome movies!" I say in mock outrage.

"I figured you would pick something a little more girly." He chuckles again as I push him with my arm.

"It's more than just fast cars! It's about love and family, even those that may not share your blood." I smile wide at him.

"Yeah, come to think of it, you're right. Crazy how they can intertwine that into a movie about criminals with fast cars." He says, pressing the remote to start the movie.

Brian

At some point during the movie we lay down on the couch together, getting into a more comfortable position. She feels so right lying against me.

Lightly running my finger tips down the length of her arm, I watch as goosebumps pop up along her silky smooth skin.

I can't stop myself from kissing the shell of her ear eliciting a sigh from her lips. Running my nose along her throat, I breathe in her scent.

"You always smell like coconuts." I whisper to her.

"You always smell like the rain." She whispers back, turning her face towards my own.

I waste no time taking her mouth with my own, reaching up with my right hand to cup the side of her head. Without pulling away, I feel her shift her back around to face me, bringing us closer together.

There's no way she can miss the hardness behind my zipper as she pushes further into me causing a groan to escape my throat.

"Maybe we should stop now." I pull back to whisper to her, looking deep into her shining eyes.

"I don't want to stop." She whispers back.

"I need you to be sure Becky. I would never forgive myself if you felt pressured into anything." I grab her face, making sure she knows how serious I am about this.

"I'm sure Brian. I need you." She moans, pressing her core against my hard cock again.

Raising up from the couch, I quickly scoop her up into my arms and head towards my bedroom.

"I can walk, you know." She giggles at me.

"Maybe I did it to keep you from running. I mean it did take entirely too long to get you to go out with me." I huff, rolling my own eyes. She laughs even harder at me.

"I'm not running now." She finally says, reaching up to nibble at my own ear and I can't wait to get her naked to lick every inch of her body.

I set her down next to my giant bed and reach to pull her dress over her head. What I reveal completely knocks out every wet dream I have had of her by far.

"Damn. I love black lace." I barely get out before my mouth swoops down taking her nipple through the delicate looking fabric.

I suck as hard as I can, causing her head to lay back and moans come from her mouth. My cock jumps in my jeans reminding me that we are still too overdressed.

Letting her nipple go with a pop, I gently help her to sit on the bed while I fumble to take all of my clothes off, finally letting my hard member jump free from its confines. She gasps at the sight of me.

"I didn't know you have tattoos." She says, looking at them as best she can in the dim light of the room.

"They are all well hidden under my clothes. Most don't know that I have them unless I'm in my swim trunks. Now, back to what I was doing." My last statement has her face going red.

I'm sure the look on my face appears like a predator ready to feast on his prey. The woman of my dreams is giving herself to me and I plan to take my time worshipping her beautiful body.

I slowly crawl up her body, starting my kisses with her calves. As I get closer to her center, her breathing escalates.

Still not taking her sexy little panties off, I lick up the front of them pressing hard with my tongue. Her hands move to my head as her mouth forms a silent O.

I reach to pull the lacey underwear down her thighs, slowly following them down with gentle kisses until they are completely gone.

Without any warning to her, my mouth latches on to her clit, sucking it into my mouth as my tongue vibrates against it.

"Oh God." She moans out, grabbing my head again to keep me in place. Not that I wanted to leave from where I was anyway.

Within seconds, she's coming all over my mouth. I lick her through it all as she comes back down. Letting her go for only a moment, I reach for a condom in my nightstand.

I had bought them earlier in the day telling myself they were something I needed just in case. I had debated with myself over buying them because I didn't want her to think I was pushing her into it. Now, I'm glad that we have them.

Putting it on quickly, I slide up her body running my length through her juices and along her now sensitive clit.

She reaches down with her little hand, lining me up with her center as I slowly ease into her.

It's a tight fit that feels like absolute heaven. I start out very slowly, listening to her sounds of pleasure as I hit a certain spot deep within her.

"Faster Brian." She whispers, taking my mouth with her own.

I pump into her harder, feeling every time I hit that spot of hers causing her to claw my back harder and her core to tighten on my cock.

"Come for me baby." I whisper, kissing her deeply again.

She moans into my mouth as I feel her core go tighter than before. My body recognising that she's coming, my cock twitches once more before I release all I've got with a roar.

We lay connected for several long minutes before I get up to get rid of the condom. When I come back to the bed, she's fast asleep. Pulling her close to me, I cover us both with the blanket and fall asleep with her in my arms.

Chapter 7
Becky

I wake to the smell of breakfast being cooked and voices in the kitchen. Turning to Brian's side of the bed, I see that he is still asleep next to me. With my heart beating quickly, I gently shake him awake.

"Brian, someone's in the kitchen!" I whisper to him.

He raises his head, listening for a few seconds before laying his head back down.

"It's just my parents." He says, trying to pull me closer.

"You're parents? Oh my god, what if they see us like this?" I begin to panic, climbing from the bed to hunt for my clothes until I hear him laughing at me. "Why are you laughing? This is serious!" I look at him wondering if he's gone mad.

He gets out of the bed in his glorious naked state, walking over to me before wrapping his arms around me and kissing my nose.

"We aren't teenagers that need to hide. Besides, my parents already know about you." He says, walking towards the bathroom.

He doesn't understand that his statement is what truly bothers me. What if they know about all the rumors that circle around this town about me? They will hate me for sure.

Trying to hold back tears at the thought. I get dressed quickly. Looking at myself in the mirror, I sigh at the wrinkled state my dress is in.

Brian walks back out of the bathroom, heading towards the closet.

"Do you have a pair of sweats I could borrow and a t-shirt?" I ask, bringing his eyes back to me.

"You can borrow anything I have, sweetheart. Check the drawers over there. Should be some sweats in the top drawer and my shirt's are hanging in the closet." He answers.

He comes right back out a few minutes later wearing a pair of jeans and a tight fitting black shirt.

"Come to the kitchen when you are ready." He hugs me to him, kissing me deeply before heading out the door.

I take my time, in no rush to face his parents who may already dislike me.

"Will life ever be easier?" I ask out loud knowing full well that life is never easy.

Brian

I find both of my parents in the kitchen. Mom of course is at the stove making breakfast while dad stands next to her trying to sneak bacon when she isn't looking.

"I thought you two weren't going to get here until later today?" I ask with a smile, grabbing their attention.

"There's my sweet boy." My moves to hug me and dad takes the opportunity to stuff more bacon pieces into his mouth.

"If you don't stop stealing all the bacon, there isn't going to be enough for that sweet young lady once she comes out of that room." Mom says to dad with her hands on her hips.

"There's plenty, woman! Surely she isn't going to eat five pounds of bacon on her own." Dad says with his mouth full pointing to the plate that is piled high with it.

I just laugh, shaking my head at them.

"And how exactly do the two of you know that she is even here?" I ask, grabbing a cup to get some coffee that I am sure dad made.

"That car in the driveway. Plus her purse is on the table." Mom points over to where it sits and I can't help the grin.

She's better at noticing things than a detective who's been on the job for twenty years.

"I think she's a little nervous to come out. Hearing you two in here seemed to scare the daylights out of her." I take a seat at the kitchen island on a stool.

"Well, most of us are harmless. I am anyway, I can't really speak for your mom." Dad grumbles as she swats his hand with a spoon.

"Hello." We all hear from the door.

"There she is! I hope you are hungry. I fixed a little bit of everything. There's coffee too. Let me grab you a cup." My mom is all smiles, flitting around as if she is the one that should be nervous.

My girl looks a little shell shocked watching my mom gush all over her. I just sit there sipping my coffee, smiling as I watch.

I told her there really wasn't anything to worry about with my parents. They are the best people you could ever meet.

Becky

Breakfast is amazing with Brian's parents. They are such sweet people. I'm completely worried about them hearing the rumors about me while here this weekend.

I'm actually surprised Brian hasn't said anything about them since meeting me. Maybe he hasn't heard them yet although that is highly unlikely.

"What time do you have to be at work?" Brian asks me as we are finishing up breakfast.

"In about an hour." I answer, looking at the clock on the wall. "I only have to be there for the lunch hour."

"I can pick up Max for practice later. Don't forget that we have dinner tonight to celebrate with the team for the start of a new season." Brian says, carrying his plate to the sink.

"Oh I can't wait to meet all of your players, son. Kids are so much fun." His mom smiles at him.

My heart trips at the thought that they will be there tonight as well as Karen and her cronies. I have to get this out in the open with them.

"I need to tell you all something." Three pairs of eyes turn my way expectantly.

"Is something the matter dear?" Mr. Lewis asks.

"I'm afraid that you all might hear some things tonight. Things about me that may alter the way you think of me. And I want to just tell you all about myself now and save myself the heart ache later." I gulp down, lifting my eyes to look at them one by one.

"Babe.." Brian starts towards me but I hold my hands up to stop him.

"Just let me get it all out first. Okay?" I ask, looking at him pleadingly until he shakes his head.

"Go ahead sweetheart, we are all listening but just so you know, nothing will alter the way we think of you. Our son obviously has strong feelings for you and that is good enough for us." Mrs. Lewis smiles gently at me waiting for me to continue.

"My family has never been looked at kindly in this town. My mom. Ugh. My mom!" I shake my head at the thought of her. "She was a really bad drunk when I was growing up. Most nights she never even came home from the bar. Usually because she found some man to take her home for a night or two. In a small town like this, you can't hide that kind of thing." I take a deep breath, sitting back down in my chair at the table.

"The kids always picked on me. Especially about my clothes. Martha, from the diner, started noticing me one day just hanging out at the park by myself. She started coming there every day after school and would share her lunch with me. I know now that she always packed extra just for me on purpose. Eventually she started getting me to meet her at the diner. Harry, her husband, would help me with my homework. The two of them would even buy my clothes." I smile as the memories of those two flood my brain.

"They sound like amazing people. We can't wait to meet them." Mr. Lewis says, patting his wife's hand who seems to have tears in her eyes.

"They are amazing. I don't know where I'd be now if it weren't for them." I swallow hard. "By the last year of highschool. I figured I would never be accepted. Then one day a boy at school started noticing me. Going out of his way to talk to me. We started seeing each other outside of school but never with his friends. I didn't think much about it then. I should have.

By the time I figured out it was all just a huge joke, I was pregnant with Max. He didn't want anyone to know about him and I, so he started the rumors about me sleeping around until everyone believed it." I stop, taking a sip of my water.

Looking up into Brian's eyes I see sympathy and anger as well. Knowing the anger is not directed at me makes my heart swell. *I'm falling in love with him.* I think to myself as I wipe the tears from my eyes that I hadn't realized had begun to fall.

"The night Max was born, this boy showed up at the hospital with his dad demanding a rapid DNA test. It was back within hours and only an hour after that I was handed papers that showed he had signed away his rights to our son as well as a non-disclosure agreement. I was warned to never let it be known who he was or I could lose my baby. So I stayed quiet. Never telling a soul." I look back up, tears falling once again.

"Mayor Hall." Brian quietly says.

I stay quiet, not giving a direct answer although he doesn't need one. Anyone with eyes in their head can see who Max's dad is if they chose to look close enough.

"So for thirteen years you have stayed quiet while they treat you like scum? Not my future daughter in law! Not any more." Mrs. Lewis slaps her hand on the table making me jump with her outburst.

Did she say future daughter in law? I ask myself, trying to catch back up with the conversation.

"You my dear, don't deserve what you have been through. I know from my son and from talking to you this morning that you are an amazing young lady. A strong woman that has persevered regardless of what life has thrown her way. Stop feeling like we would ever think any differently of you." Mrs. Lewis says, walking over to my side, wrapping her arms around me.

I hug her back, truly hopeful for the first time in my entire life.

Chapter 8
Brian

We had an amazing practice after everyone was told who made the team. While I wanted so badly to cut Luke from the team, I couldn't do so. He's a good player but needs to work on being a team player. Maybe it's not too late to change the way his parents have made him to be.

We all get to Gamez Pizza afterwards, the kids running around everywhere trying to play every game they possibly can. I paid for everything ahead of time so that the kids wouldn't need tokens for the night.

"You are doing great with those boys. I'm proud of you, son." My dad says, slapping my back.

"Thanks, Dad. I'm going to enjoy it. It was something I always wanted to do anyway."

"I remember. You always said that if you didn't make it in the league you would just coach. But I have to say, while you were an amazing player, I think you are an outstanding coach." He smiles as I lean in to hug him.

"You are a great dad, you know that?" I ask.

"Hey, I'm right here too!" Mom exclaims from the other side. I smile in her direction.

"You already know you are the best mom in the whole world." I smile as her face beams with pride.

Looking over at Becky, I see her getting up from her chair.

"Where are you off to?" I ask.

"Just going to the ladies room. I'll be back in a few minutes." She smiles back as I watch her walk away.

"I have to say, I really do like her." Mom says with a grin.

"I really like her too." I murmur back.

"When are you going to pop the question?" Dad looks at me expectantly to see how I answer mom's newest question.

"I'm not sure. I think I need a ring first though." I answer after a minute.

"Well, I figured as much so I brought this with me." She smiles widely again as she pulls a small box from her purse and opens it.

"Grandma's ring?" I ask with surprise.

"Well it's not like I have a daughter to pass it down to so a daughter in law will have to do." She states simply.

If I didn't already love my mom with all my whole heart, I would right this minute. My parents really are the best parents in the entire world.

Grabbing my mom in a hard hug, I hold her to me.

"I love you, mom." I whisper.

"I love you too, sweet boy. Now hurry up. I need to legally, be able to spoil my grandson." She pushes me back to look into my eyes as I laugh at her statement.

Becky

Finishing up in the bathroom, I head out the door but the door hits something. I hear what sounds like liquid hitting the floor as someone gasps. *Shit.*

Looking around the door, I see Karen standing there with wet clothes as a cup rolls around the floor. *Double shit.*

"I'm so sorry Karen." I say.

"Sorry? You're sorry? You did this shit on purpose!" She accuses me.

"You are mistaken. There's no way I knew you were that close to the door." I explain with exasperation.

"Bullshit! You did it on purpose because you hate me! You've hated me ever since highschool because James wouldn't have you!" Her screeching has started to draw attention our way as a crowd starts to form.

"Why would I hate you? Especially over James? He's not worthy of my damn attention! Never was!" I yell back, starting to have enough of her shit.

"He's an amazing man. Loves me and our son. The most honourable man in this whole town." She seems to swell with pride at that statement.

"Honourable? Ha! He's the most untrustworthy man in this town! You think he tells the truth every time his mouth opens. Do you have any idea where he spends Friday nights? I bet you have no clue!" I exclaim.

"What are you talking about? My husband would never lie to me!" She answers back but I see doubt in her eyes.

"You really think so?" I ask, crossing my arms over my chest. "Have you never really looked at my son? I mean really locked at him and then looked at your husband?" I huff, rolling my eyes.

"James can't be Max's father." She crosses her arms and shakes her head. If I could take a picture of how wide her eyes are, I'd cherish that shit forever.

"Why do you say that Karen? Because he told everyone that I was sleeping with truck drivers coming into town? You are ridiculous. I'm done with this conversation." I step around her, walking back through the crowd in search of Brian and his parents.

I probably shouldn't have done that but I have had enough. I'm tired of being treated like shit all because of a rumor her own husband started as if being the child of my own mother wasn't bad enough growing up.

As I come through the crowd, I notice Max standing off to the side looking back at me and my heart sinks knowing he might have heard some of that.

Walking over to him, I kneel down to look into his eyes.

"Max, were you listening just now?" I ask, heart hammering.

"Yeah. But it's okay mom." He smiles, pulling me in for a hug.

"It's okay?" I ask with wonder.

"Yeah, it's fine. I already knew anyway." He pulls back, shrugging his shoulders.

"How did you already know? I made sure to never tell anyone." I ask with concern.

"Luke let it slip one day at school. He was trying to be mean telling me that our dad would never love me as much as he loved him. I told him that man could never be my dad. He's too mean." He states with a firm shake of his head.

I can't contain the laugh that escapes at the thought of him telling Luke just that.

"Let's go find Brian and his parents." I smile down at my son so very thankful to have him in my life.

Brian

I watch as Becky walks up with Max at her side. Both have huge smiles as they get to the table.

"Everything okay?" I ask, kissing her cheek.

"Everything is great. Today has been an amazing day. And it's all thanks to you." She says, looking at me.

"Really? Well maybe I can make it even better than great." I say.

"What do you mean?" She asks then gasps as I get down on one knee in front of her, holding the ring up with one hand.

"Becky. You are the most beautiful woman I have ever met. All I want to do is give you everything I've got. My heart. My soul. My body. My earthly possessions. If there's ever anything we don't already have, I will walk over fire to get it for you if that is your desire. My only desire is for you to be my wife. I want nothing else in this life but you. Will you marry me?" She has tears streaming down her face now. Her hands covering her mouth.

Her head starts to shake yes before she ever utters a word.

"Yes." She whispers then louder. "Yes. A thousand times yes!" She exclaims, falling into my arms.

Holding her close while I push the ring onto her finger I hear a crowd around us as they begin to clap and cheer with congratulations.

I meant every word I said. I want nothing more than to give her all I've got. Forever.

The End

* * *

Enjoy this story? Be sure to leave a review!

* * *

About the Author

Marissa Ann spends her time in rural North Mississippi with her husband, the kids and all of their animals on a hobby farm.

She always said she would write books one day even though many thought she never would. She made a promise to a childhood friend who left this world for the next in 2015. That she would finally write and publish at least one.

Her first book hit the market in 2018 and she's never looked back. She now has several out with many more scheduled for release. Want to stay up to date with new releases, giveaways and all the cool things?

Sign up for Marissa's newsletter here: **https://www.authormarissaann.com/** or join **Marissa Ann Romance Readers** on Facebook.

Keep reading for a sneak peak at Poison Pen Book 1, Baratta's Darkness

Poison Pen
Baratta's Darkness
Prologue
Baratta

The club is packed as I make my way to the balcony hoping to get some air. Finding a quiet spot on the far side, I sit and drink my scotch slowly while the boss finishes up his meeting inside. A few minutes goes by when a young woman walks out, stopping to look over the balcony to the street below. New Orleans is always a party town, especially on Saturday night.

She doesn't seem to notice me in the corner, but I happen to be good at blending into the shadows. My eyes are drawn to her, not just by her beauty but by the gorgeous tattoo that goes up one leg disappearing under her short skirt.

"Hey, we all are going to another bar. Want to come with us?" I hear as another woman walks up next to her.

"Nah, I think I'll call it a night soon and go back to the hotel. My flight leaves pretty early." She responds in a sultry husky voice that immediately has me wondering what she would sound like with her legs wrapped around my head.

She stays in the exact same spot for several more minutes after the other girl leaves. As she turns around, she finally notices me as she jumps a little bit and her hand goes to her chest.

"I'm sorry. I didn't see you there." She smiles in my direction.

"I wasn't really trying to be seen." I respond as I take another sip of my scotch.

"Well, sorry." She says as she turns to leave.

"Where are you running off to?" I ask, not really wanting her to leave which is completely out of character for me.

"Back to my hotel. I have an early flight." She smiles again and I catch my breath at her beauty yet again.

What the fuck is wrong with me? I think to myself. I am never impulsive. I calculate everything.

"So you are not from around here then?" I grin back at her as I lean forward, more into the light. I watch as her smile becomes even bigger.

Maybe I won't have to go very far for a fuck tonight after all. Something about this woman has my dick harder than a nail and I don't even know her name.

I convince her to hang out a bit longer. I can't leave until my boss is done with his meeting but I don't tell her that. I offer to buy her a drink instead. I know Uncle Tony won't mind if I slip away after he gets out of here.

Yeah, my boss is also my Uncle. He runs the Italian mob in Louisiana. When my mom died, Uncle Tony and Aunt Morgania took me in. My twin brother went to live with our Grandparents in Italy.

It isn't more than a few minutes later when I see Uncle's bodyguards pushing their way out the front door. He looks up, nodding at me before slipping into his waiting car. The rest of the night is mine. I know exactly where I am going to spend it, or maybe I should say who I am going to spend it in.

Fiona

Today was a huge success for my business. Accepting the invitation to the Inkers Expo they were holding this year in New Orleans was the best decision I could have made. There were so many big names in the business here that would be able to get my name out there. There were several reporters that stopped to take pictures and ask questions about my work.

My dreams were coming true and I had my brother to thank for that. He and his club, The Wolfsbane Ridge MC, gave me my first loan to open up shop after they realized how much I loved to draw and eventually do tattoos. I don't use stencils to do my work, everything is by hand.

Finished with cleanup at my station, I begin packing all of my supplies back into my duffle bags when a couple of the girls I met here walk up asking if I want to go to the after party with them. I think it would be fun, plus hopefully another chance to meet some more people in the business with connections.

"Whew! They are so packed tonight!" Lilyanna comments as we scan for an area to sit.

"Look, there's Clint with some of the others. Let's go up there." Ashley points to the balcony above where there are less people but more of the crowd from the Inkers Expo.

A couple hours later, I decide to get some air as I excuse myself from my friends and head outside. I look out over the street below at all the people walking around and having fun. Some I know are tourists as they stop every so often to take pictures.

I haven't taken a single moment to do the tourist thing. I'm out of time now since I leave tomorrow. Hopefully I can come again just to visit and look around without worrying about work. I think to myself as I watch everyone below.

"Hey, we all are going to another bar. Want to come with us?" asks Ashley as she comes up behind me.

"Nah, I think I'll call it a night soon and go back to the hotel. My flight leaves pretty early."

"Have a safe trip and don't forget about all your new friends now." She says with a smile.

I hug her as we say goodbye. Looking back out over the street below I think about all the new connections this week has brought me. I am truly excited to get back home and get started on all the new bookings I have for next week.

As I turn around a guy in the corner catches my eye and I jump a little not expecting to see anyone. Has he been there the whole time? I ask myself.

I smile to be polite at the handsome stranger but when he steps out into the light. Oh My God! My panties drop and I let loose a real smile. This man could probably rock my world. I want!

I've never had a one night stand before but I think that is about to change, there is no way I am letting this guy get away without revealing that impressive bulge I can see straining against his pants.

"Hi, I am Fiona, but my friends all call me Fee." I tell him as I extend my hand for a shake.

"Baratta" he says and when he reaches out to shake my hand I check for a wedding ring. No ring, my clit is doing a happy dance. Good thing we are standing, my panties are so wet now, sitting would be uncomfortable.

Chapter 1
Fiona

I grew up in White Summer Montana but I had big dreams, I was going to see the world. First chance I got I was out of here. Turns out the world isn't that wonderful without your family at your side. So after a messy relationship ended I decided it was time to come home.

I made a name for myself. People from all around the globe came to me for tattoos. They would come to me in White Summer just like they did in Seattle.

I knew my brother's club had been having some issues but I was an outsider and always would be, it didn't bother me. He had his life and I had mine. Just being close gave me the security and comfort I need.

I know that if I ever need them the Timberwolves MC would be here for me. They even loaned me the start-up to help transfer my shop here.

On my first trip home to get the ball rolling, the club was in chaos. They had visitors from out of town. That's when I saw HIM.

It's been two years since New Orleans but I'll never forget the man that rocked my world then disappeared into thin air. After going back to my hotel we spent the night wrapped up in each other. Finally falling asleep in the early hours of dawn. I only slept a couple hours and when I woke up he was gone.

It was a good thing I had packed before going out with the girls. I barely had time to grab my stuff and get to the airport before my flight back to Seattle. I slept the entire way. I daydreamed about him often but never thought I would actually see him again. Especially not here.

He didn't even try to talk to me. I actually think he went out of his way to avoid me. Then he was gone again, like a ghost. Appearing and disappearing from my life.

Baratta

When Uncle Tony informed me that we were headed back to White Summer Montana to attend the grand opening of the Poison Pen, I felt as if I were punched in the gut.

Very similar to the way I felt when our eyes connected that day several months ago when she came strolling into the Wolfsbane Ridge club house.

Finding out that her brother was the sergeant at arms for the club whose girls had been kidnapped and sold into trafficking by Joey, surprised the hell out of me. And I don't like fucking surprises!

I tried to make excuses as to why I should stay in New Orleans but none of them worked. Uncle Tony was going to relent but Aunt Morgania got that little shit eating grin on her face right before she told Uncle that she would only feel completely safe if I were there with them.

So here I am at the airport loading our bags into the rental car as Uncle calls to check on our reservations at Wolf's Ridge which is owned by the club.

"Our cabins are ready for us. After we drop off our luggage you can leave me at the clubhouse. I have a meeting scheduled with Timber. I think your Aunt wants you to take her into town." Uncle Tony looks over at my Aunt with raised brows.

"Yes please. If it's not too much trouble for you Baratta. All the girls are at Bella's Brew."

"It's not a problem Aunty." I say while looking at her through the rearview mirror which makes her smile.

Calling her Aunty in private has always put a smile on her face. No one outside our family knows the truth of who I am. I prefer it that way so that those I love can not be used against me.

The kind of work that I am in comes with hazards that can get my family killed. Hell, it can get me killed. I don't worry about any of that though. I have zero guilt when it comes to putting a bullet into someone. I actually never think of them again.

While I don't feel shit when it comes to others, I know my rage would take over if anything happened to my Aunt and Uncle. My cousin too.

I'm really fond of Markayla. She was always really sweet to me when we were younger. The other kids and even the teachers treated me like shit. They said something was wrong with me.

Especially after the day I hit another kid in the head with a rock busting his head open. He had pushed Markayla down on the playground making her knee bleed. I refused to say I was sorry for what I did to him because hell, I wasn't sorry at all.

All these years later and I'm still not sorry.

Fiona

I didn't sleep at all last night, today is opening day at Poison Pen. It's still early so I am sitting at the counter at Bella's coffee shop. I thought it would calm me down but it's just adding to my already frazzled nerves.

Bella and Mina are sitting on either side of me, for moral support. Bella is sucking down coffee like it's going out of style. I suppose having two babies at home, she needs the caffeine. Victory is a newborn and Justice is teething.

I am just about to ask where Miranda and Hayden are, when they come walking in the door. "Speak of the devil." I say instead.

"Huh?" They both look at me.

"I was just about to ask about the two of you." I reply as they join us.

Hayden orders a coffee from Bella's mom but Miranda just asks for water. We all turn to look at her; she immediately gives us a shy grin.

"Well you know how me and Blood decided to try for a baby? My doctor said caffeine is bad for him or her." She says with a sly grin. It takes a minute for her meaning to sink into my already frazzled nerves but then I understand.

"OH MY GOD!" I scream, "I am going to be an Aunt!"

We all jump up surrounding Miranda, all of us giving her congratulations and hugs. When it's my turn I wrap my arms around my new sister and burst into tears. Now everybody is hugging me instead.

The words, "don't cry" make it through my sobbing but I explain they are happy tears.

"I am just so happy. Today I open my new shop and find out I have a new niece or nephew on the way. There is nothing that can ruin my day now."

Maybe I spoke too soon.

Baratta

I drop off my Uncle at the Wolfsbane clubhouse so he can meet with Timber and the guys. They still have some things to work out. Uncle Tony asked me to drive Aunt Morgania to Bella's Brew where the girls are supposed to be hanging out today.

Through the window I watch as Morgania joins the women. Delilah, Bella's mom, is serving customers and refilling coffee cups. I'm about to go sit in the car where I can watch them without being in the way when Fiona turns to look out the window.

I immediately notice her red eyes and tear streaked face. Something about her kicks my protective instincts into overdrive and I storm into the shop ready to kill whatever has caused such distress to her. Before I even think about what I am doing I grab her chin so she can't look away.

"What's wrong? Why are you crying? Did someone hurt you?" The questions just fly out of my mouth and then she starts laughing.

My hands drop and I step back. A minute ago she was balling her eyes out and now she is laughing? She is laughing … at me. Dear Lord, she is insane. Going from one extreme to the other, what the hell have I walked into? I look around at Bella, Mina, Miranda and that Hayden chick that runs the local gym and they are all laughing.

My Aunt pushes me to the side and hugs Fiona. "What's wrong, dear?"

"Nothing is wrong. These are happy tears. I am going to be an Aunt." she says as she wipes her eyes one more time.

Aunt Morgania looks at each of the women one at a time, and they all shake their heads. Until she gets to Miranda, who nods.

I feel a weight lift off my chest. When did I care so much about this woman's tears? I barely know her yet I was ready to kill whoever made her cry. I start to back out of the store but Morgania stops me to ask if I'll go with Fiona over to her shop so she can prepare for opening.

I try to convince Aunt Morgania that I need to stay and protect her but she looks at the women and says, "Who is packing." every hand in the group goes up. I know when I am outnumbered. So I concede by asking Fiona if she is ready to go.

Fiona

Why the fuck is he here? I think to myself as he holds the passenger side door open for me. I knew the club had extended the invitation to Mr. Marcus and we girls have stayed in touch with Morgania so naturally we expected them. But did they honestly have to bring him along?

I know that I am being a little petty. He seems to be their body guard or something. I've never really asked what exactly he does. I do know one thing for sure. The Marcus family is a well known Mob organization.

"Pull around to the back please." I point to the driveway leading to the back parking lot as we come up to the shop.

When he stops, I don't wait for him to get out and open my door. I quickly jump out and head for the building. The less time I am in his company the better.

Reaching the landing of the stairs that lead up to the attached apartment that I moved into, I hear him get out and walk across the gravel behind me.

"You don't have to come up. Thank you for the ride though." I look back at him and think that maybe I shouldn't have. My eyes are glued to his just as they were that very first night and I feel as though I can't get enough air into my lungs.

"I am sure Blood would appreciate me checking everything out before I just leave you all alone." The corner of his mouth lifts as he walks around me going up the stairs to my door.

Instead of saying anything else to the stubborn ass, I follow him up the stairs. Reaching the door I notice there is a package with my name on it. Picking it up, I take it inside with me.

"Did you really not lock the door while you were gone?" Baratta asks as he walks into the kitchen.

"This is White Summer, not Seattle or New Orleans. If anything happens here, my brother takes care of it." I shrug my shoulders as I reach to open the box that was left for me on the porch.

As it opens up, I remove the tissue paper that is on top to reveal what looks to be a cut out of me from a picture that was taken. But the picture is clearly from when I was in the shower as you can see the water running down my back. In bold black ink down my back someone has written MINE.

"What the fuck?" I breathe out as all I can do is look at it. Baratta's hand comes from beside me grabbing the cutout and examining it.

"I am going to assume that you did not willingly pose for this picture?" Baratta says through gritted teeth. I am unsure if he is pissed about the picture or the thought that I would actually willingly pose for it.

"Of course not!" As I reach out to grab the picture from him hoping to hide it, I see more writing on the back. In angry red letters it says, "Did you think you could leave me behind?"

I sink down into a chair as a cold chill seems to start at my toes and move up my body. Baratta is so busy looking at the picture and ignoring me that he doesn't even notice when I put my head between my knees and struggle to breathe.

"So, it's a threat then." He states matter of factly.

"We don't know if it's a threat. There isn't a note in the box." I snap back. I don't know if it's his attitude, his presence or what it is but just seconds ago I was on the verge of a panic attack. Now I just want to hit him and make him leave.

"You are not naive Fi, so don't act like it. We need to let your brother and his club know about this."

"Absolutely not! There is no need to get them involved just yet. We don't even know what this is anyway."

I know I should do what he says and tell my family. However; I'm still hurt by the way he left me in New Orleans and especially pissed about him just disappearing the last time he was here without so much as a word.

"Okay. If you don't want to tell them then the only thing left to do is for me to stay here with you. I will let Uncle know and we can go pick up my suitcase from the cabin." He talks so calmly as if it is all settled.

"No. You are not staying here with me. And did you just say Uncle? I didn't know you brought your Uncle with you."

Baratta

Oh fuck, I have never slipped and called Tony, Uncle in front of anyone before. It's not like I can pretend I didn't say it. She clearly heard me. I run my hands over my face and through my hair in frustration. What is it about this woman that lowers all my carefully built walls?

"Listen to me and listen closely," I growl as I grab her shoulders. "Tony and Morgania are my Uncle and Aunt. You can't tell anyone! Not your brother! Not his club! Not your girl club! Nobody can know this! Not ever!"

For the first time ever Fiona looks frightened of me, but I can't let this closely guarded secret get out. Now I have to stay not just for her protection but the safety of my family as well.

I will kill to keep my family safe and for some reason my heart is including her. I'm not willing to examine that just yet. At least not out loud. She'd fight me on it. On that thought maybe I would like to voice it out loud in front of her.

I step back and look into her eyes. The fire that was missing a few minutes ago is back. She thinks I didn't notice her on the edge, I see everything. It is the way I was trained. I knew if I gave in and showed compassion she would be a sobbing mess.

I prefer when my woman fights with me and next to me. I don't want her to be a delicate little flower. She doesn't know it yet but this little gift just sealed the deal. She is mine and I am not leaving her again.

Other Titles by Marissa Ann

Wolfsbane Ridge MC Series
Book 1 Timber's Fairy
https://books2read.com/TimbersFairy

Book 2 Blade's Pixie
https://books2read.com/BladesPixie

Book 3 Blood's Angel
https://books2read.com/BloodsAngel

Book 4 Wrench's Salvation
https://books2read.com/WrenchsSalvation

Book 5 Bear's Saviour
https://books2read.com/BearsSaviour

Book 6 Torque's Gaze
https://books2read.com/TorquesGaze

Night Howler's MC, Mississippi
Book 1 Chucky's Pride
https://books2read.com/Chuckys-Pride

Book 2 Reaper's Jewels
https://books2read.com/ReapersJewels

Night Howler's MC Series, New Orleans
Book 1 Buzz
https://books2read.com/BuzzNewOrleans

Book 2 Skeeter
https://books2read.com/Skeeter

Poison Pen Series
Book 1 Baratta's Darkness
https://books2read.com/BarattasDarkness

Book 2 Lily's Shadow
https://books2read.com/LilysShadow

Book 3 Arin's Light
https://books2read.com/ArinsLight

Connect with the Author

Website:

www.authormarissaann.com

Facebook:

https://www.facebook.com/MarissaAnnAuthor

Instagram:

https://www.instagram.com/authormarissaann/

Twitter:

https://twitter.com/marissaannbooks

Goodreads:

https://www.goodreads.com/author/show/18159855.Marissa_Ann

Linkedin:

https://www.linkedin.com/in/marissa-ann-ballard-93982b186/

Tik Tok

https://www.tiktok.com/@authormarissaann

Thank you for reading!

You may write to Marissa Ann at:
admin@authormarissaann.com OR

Author Marissa Ann
PO Box 833
Belmont, Mississippi 38827

9 781736 579893